Baba Yaga and Vasilisa the Brave

As told by

Marianna Mayer

Illustrated by

K. Y. Craft

MORROW JUNIOR BOOKS / NEW YORK

Watercolor, gouache, and oil were used for the full-color illustrations.
The text type is 18-point Nicholas Cochin Roman.

Library of Congress Cataloging-in-Publication Data
Mayer, Marianna.
Baba Yaga and Vasilisa the Brave / by Marianna Mayer; illustrated by Kinuko Y. Craft.   p. cm.
Summary: A retelling of the old Russian fairy tale in which beautiful Vasilisa uses the help of her doll to escape from the clutches of the witch Baba Yaga, who in turn sets in motion the events which lead to the once ill-treated girl's marrying the tzar.
ISBN 0-688-08500-8 (trade) — ISBN 0-688-08501-6 (library)
[1. Fairy tales.   2. Folklore — Soviet Union.]   I. Craft, Kinuko, ill.   II. Title.
PZ8.M4514Bab   1994   398.21'0947—dc20   90-38514   CIP   AC

to DENNIS LOMBARDI ❊ m. m. ❊

to WOLFGANG ✱ K. y. c. ✱

eep in the birch forest, in a small clearing, lives the ancient, the terrible Baba Yaga. No one knows how old she is; she has always been there in the forest.

Baba Yaga is very tall, and thin as a skeleton, though she never stops eating. Humans are Baba Yaga's favorite food, and she is always hungry. Indeed, her crooked hut is made of human bones, evidence of her numerous meals.

It should be no wonder, then, that Baba Yaga lives alone. Even so, from time to time, there is the occasional visitor, the stray traveler, the hapless wanderer. Few have survived the visit. However, there was one in particular, a young girl, whose encounter with Baba Yaga bears repeating. This is how it happened.

t the far edge of **B**aba **Y**aga's forest there lived a mean-spirited woman with her two ill-tempered daughters and her stepdaughter, **V**asilisa. **W**hereas the other girls were cruel and ugly, **V**asilisa was kindness itself and beautiful beyond measure.

Vasilisa's mother had died when the girl was quite young. **H**er father had soon remarried, more for the child's sake than for his own, believing his daughter should have a mother's love as she grew up. **B**ut while his intentions were for the good, the results were sadly the opposite.

It was not many years later that he, too, passed away, leaving the orphaned **V**asilisa at the mercy of her stepmother. **W**hile he was alive, the woman pretended affection where there was none, but once free of her husband, she allowed herself to behave as she pleased. **A**ll his wealth was entrusted to the stepmother with the understanding that she would take care of **V**asilisa. **I**nstead, she indulged her two daughters' every whim and made **V**asilisa's life as miserable as possible.

he orphan was banished to the coldest, darkest part of the house and given every menial task to do. The stepsisters followed their mother's example and delighted in teasing the poor girl when they were not also ordering her to do their bidding. It was, *"Oh, you lazy girl, why hasn't the floor been scrubbed yet?"* And, *"When will you finish with the cooking so you can do the washing up?"*

Vasilisa would have asked for mercy, had there been anyone to listen. Certainly she would have run away, had there been anywhere to go. Sadly there was not. And so she might have grown bitter, and her sweet nature might have turned cold and hard. But for Vasilisa, cruelty made her more kind and compassionate. It seemed an inner voice guided her and gave her strength, and then, if this was not enough, she had a special treasure that made all else bearable.

t was a doll made by her mother just a few months before she died. All her mother's love had gone into the making of that doll. When it was finished, her mother told her, "If ever you are in need, this doll will comfort you." And, in truth, by some miracle the doll did.

In other ways it was a plain and simple doll. Indeed, the stepsisters would never have owned such an ordinary one. But Vasilisa kept it near her always; it was her secret.

Most astonishing of all, the doll was *alive*.

At night when Vasilisa was left to the darkness of her shabby quarters, she would pour out all her hopes and dreams to this small creature. The doll would listen, her eyes glowing like embers; and quietly, so that no one else could hear, she would whisper loving words of comfort and advice.

To have such a treasure made Vasilisa's days seem shorter, caused her work to seem lighter, and gave her a sense that she was not alone in the world.

oon enough the years passed. The stepsisters reached marriageable age, and so did the beautiful Vasilisa.

Her presence seemed to make the other girls appear even more homely and dull-witted. The stepmother knew that she would never find husbands for her daughters unless she was first rid of Vasilisa.

With that in mind she devised a sinister plan. Early one evening she gave each girl a task. By the light from the flame of a single candle, her daughters were to work at their lacemaking, and Vasilisa was to do the mending.

Without complaint all three girls huddled in the small pool of light cast by the single candle and began their tasks. Beyond the light everything was in shadow, and as the hours ticked by the darkness of the night deepened and closed in to envelop the rest of the house.

The girls worked in silence, the only sound the incessant creaking of the stepmother's rocking chair as she rocked back and forth, back and forth, her catlike eyes fixed on Vasilisa.

ear midnight the candle had burned down to a tiny stub. At last the clock began to strike. At the stroke of twelve the flaming wick began to sputter, then flared and flickered, and finally went out. Suddenly the household was thrown into total darkness. The girls rushed to light a fresh candle, but their attempts failed. Indeed, they were unable to strike even a single match. A powerful spell had fallen over the house. The stepmother had planned it so, for she was a witch.

In the darkness no one could see the evil smile of satisfaction upon her lips. "Vasilisa," she ordered, "don't just stand there! Make yourself useful. Go at once to Baba Yaga's house at the other end of the forest and tell her she must lend us a light, or how shall we manage?"

Obediently Vasilisa went to her room to prepare for the long journey. The doll was waiting for her. In the dark the creature's eyes shone like two burning candles.

"Vasilisa, you look so troubled," said the doll. "Tell me what's wrong."

"My stepmother has ordered me to fetch a light from Baba Yaga. You know I shall never return."

"Listen to me, child," said the doll. "Don't despair. You must be brave. Do as your stepmother has told you, but take me with you."

t was well past midnight when Vasilisa left the house and set out across the forest. She followed a narrow footpath, and lighting her way was a full moon that seemed to drift along with her. But when she dared look beyond the path, haunting shadows shifted with the chilly wind, playing tricks with every dark shape. Shivering, Vasilisa hugged her doll closer to her heart and continued on her way.

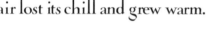he night wore on, and the moon faded.

Suddenly a pale horseman came riding on a tall white stallion and crossed the path right before Vasilisa. She saw that his face was ghostly white, as was his armor. In the next instant he disappeared, and in his wake a silvery thread of light broke through the trees. Day was dawning. A bird sang out.

The forest came to life, and Vasilisa's heart felt lighter as the last traces of night vanished. Not long after, a second rider galloped across her path. His face was sunburnt, his armor scarlet, and his horse a flame red chestnut. The sun rose behind him, and a rosy glow spread across the forest. The air lost its chill and grew warm.

he rest of the day Vasilisa walked on. Then, as the light faded and long shadows gathered, she came to a clearing. What she saw was fearsome, for there stood a high fence made of bleached bones, and on each fencepost a hollow-eyed skull sat glaring. The gate was also made of bones, the latch was a sharp-toothed mouth, and the bolt was a skeleton's hand. On the other side of the fence stood Baba Yaga's hut on its rickety stilts of bones. Vasilisa let out a breath; no one was home.

At that moment a black-cloaked horseman riding a jet black steed passed like a silent shadow. As he vanished, darkness fell, the skulls upon the fence lit up, and each pair of empty eyes burned with a fierce light. Night had arrived, and the forest was still as death.

hen, far in the distance, Vasilisa heard twigs snapping and leaves rustling. The sounds drew closer and closer, and suddenly out of the dark wood came Baba Yaga riding a mortar, swinging a pestle in one hand and her broom in the other. Down she swept before the gate, her eyes searching, her nose twitching.

"I know you're hiding there in the birches," she announced in a deep, gruff voice. "Come out at once, or I shall come and get you!"

Vasilisa felt for the little doll beneath her shawl. The small creature was still there. Vasilisa took a deep breath and stepped into the open. She bowed respectfully, and, keeping her eyes fixed on the ground, she said, "It is I, Vasilisa. My stepmother has sent me to ask if we may borrow a light."

"Is that so," replied Baba Yaga with a sly smile. "Yes, I know of your stepmother—and your stepsisters, too. You might have wished for better relations, my dear. Well, never mind. You shall have your light and you may even live to use it. We shall see. But first you must live here and work for me."

urning from the girl, Baba Yaga addressed the lock. "Open up, I say!"

Instantly the lock did as she commanded. Baba Yaga passed through the gate and, making her way up the ladder, entered the hut. Vasilisa hurried to follow. In a flash the gate slammed behind her, there was a clatter of bones, and the lock snapped shut.

When Vasilisa entered the hut, Baba Yaga was already sitting in her chair by the fire. Her black eyes sparkled as she fixed them on the girl. "I'm hungry!" she growled. "Pull out everything in the oven and serve it to me *now*."

Vasilisa did not need to be asked twice. She slipped the doll into her pocket and got to work. Inside the oven there was a twelve-foot-long baked sturgeon stuffed with wild mushrooms and *kasha*. There was a mountain of paper-thin pancakes called *blinis* in butter, a gallon of beet soup called *borscht,* and at least six dozen turnovers called *piroshki*. All this the girl served to the ravenous Baba Yaga, who ate steadily. Not once did she raise her black eyes from her plate till every last scrap was gone.

SMOKING AFTER MEALS IS ONE OF BABA YAGA'S MANY BAD HABITS...

inally the bowls and platters were empty. Baba Yaga smacked her thin lips and, wiping her mouth with her sleeve, looked up at Vasilisa.

"Tomorrow, while I'm away, I want you to take the bushel of wheat outside the hut and sort it from the chaff. Then sweep the yard, clean the hut, and don't let me find even a speck of dirt anywhere. Wash the linen and cook me a fine supper. If all this isn't done and done well, I'll have you for my supper." And with that Baba Yaga shut her eyes and began to snore.

Vasilisa sat down in a dark corner and shook her head. Silently the doll crept from her pocket. "Don't fret, child," whispered the doll. "Go to sleep now. Night is no time to solve problems. In the morning we shall see what can be done."

When Vasilisa awoke, she saw the white horseman ride through the clearing, and soon the red horseman followed. Light streamed in through the windows of the hut. It was a new day.

Baba Yaga opened her cold black eyes and whistled for her mortar and pestle. In an instant they appeared with her faithful broom. She climbed into the mortar and gave Vasilisa a smile, revealing two fine rows of long, sharp teeth. "I leave you to your work, my dear," she said, and was gone.

here to begin? thought Vasilisa. Just then the doll leaped from her pocket, ran into the yard, found the bushel, and at once set to work separating the chaff from the wheat. Vasilisa was astonished, for she had never imagined the little doll would do the tasks for her. Indeed, the little creature labored tirelessly. When she finished with the wheat, she swept the yard, scoured the hut, and laundered the linen, too.

There was nothing for Vasilisa to do but cook, and cook she did! She made cream-cheese pastries, a hot sauerkraut soup called *shchi,* and a golden bread called *coulibiac* filled with savory onion and mushrooms, salmon and rice. To be sure, she prepared many more dishes besides, so that the supper, when she finished, was a Russian feast fine enough for a tzar.

resently the black horseman rode past the hut, night drew in, the skulls upon the fence lit up, and Vasilisa heard the distant rustling that heralded Baba Yaga's return.

Then in came the tall, bony creature, her black eyes searching the hut, ready to find that the tasks were not completed. Instead she found everything spotless, the wheat separated from the chaff, and a sumptuous meal waiting.

"Did you finish?" she asked in disbelief.

"Yes," replied Vasilisa with pride. "Please sit. Your supper is ready, and you should eat while it's hot."

In spite of herself, Baba Yaga made little sounds of delight as she devoured her delicious supper. Even for her, she ate an enormous quantity. Nevertheless, at the close of the meal she said, "Since you did so well with the last set of tasks, tomorrow I shall expect that you do even more. First wash every window in the hut. Then go find the needle I lost some years ago in one of the haystacks beyond the yard. When that's been done, remove every particle of dust from the giant barrelful of poppy seeds behind the door. And of course I expect an equally splendid meal for my supper tomorrow night."

hen, after reminding the poor girl that she'd meet a
gruesome fate if she failed, Baba Yaga shut her eyes.

It might have been a sleepless night for Vasilisa,
but the doll comforted her, whispering reassuring words till the young girl fell
asleep.

The next day when Vasilisa awoke, Baba Yaga was gone. Without
delay the doll went to work, and Vasilisa began to prepare another elaborate
feast. Neither stopped until evening approached. At last, with the windows
spotless and the needle found, the doll sat down and dusted every single tiny
poppy seed.

In time the black horseman rode through the clearing, the hollow
skulls took on their unearthly light, it was nightfall again, and Baba Yaga
returned. As she surveyed the hut, she saw at
once that all the tasks had been completed and
another wonderful feast awaited her.

lmost smiling, Baba Yaga sat down to her supper and didn't stop eating until she finished everything set before her. Only then did she glance up at Vasilisa.

"You are an excellent cook, my girl," said Baba Yaga. "And quite a remarkable housekeeper. But in the area of conversation you leave much to be desired. Don't be so dull! Let me see how brave you are. Ask me a question. But, mind, not every answer I give will be to your liking."

Vasilisa gathered her courage. Somehow, tonight she felt less afraid of the terrible Baba Yaga. "There is one question I'd like to ask," said Vasilisa. "Who are the three riders that pass through the forest?"

Baba Yaga narrowed her black eyes and gave a laugh. "You are a wise one to ask only about things *outside* this hut! I don't take kindly to girls who are nosy about my private matters. Very well, I'll answer you. Those riders are my faithful knights. The white is my daybreak, the red my sun, and the black my night.

"Now it's my turn to ask a question," announced Baba Yaga gleefully. "Just how did you succeed in doing all the many tasks I set for you?"

Unwilling to conceal the truth, though she knew she might regret it, Vasilisa replied, "By my mother's love."

aba Yaga squirmed in her seat. She loathed anything to do with *love*. "Ugh!" she exclaimed. "Be off with you. It's time you took yourself home."

Getting to her feet, she shooed the girl to the door. At the gate she stopped, reminded of something. "Here, a little light for your stepmother and stepsisters," she said. Pulling one of the lighted skulls from a fencepost, Baba Yaga drove it into a stake. She handed it to the girl and pushed her out the gate, saying, "Don't forget to give this to them, my dear. Now, on your way!"

Astonished that she had escaped with her life, Vasilisa turned away from the hut and set out on her long journey across the forest. All night she walked, and the skull's gleaming eyes never failed her but kept burning like a beacon to light the way home. At daybreak the flame went out on its own. But her journey was only half over; still she walked on. Then as nightfall approached, magically the skull lit up again, aiding her for a second evening.

t last, near midnight, she arrived home. The house was pitch-black; not a candle burned in any window. It is late, thought the girl. Perhaps they are all sleeping. Thinking that her stepmother would have no use for light at this hour, she started to leave it outside.

Suddenly the skull spoke in a commanding voice. "Take me inside, Vasilisa. Baba Yaga meant you to give me to your stepmother and stepsisters. She will be very cross if you disobey."

"Very well," said Vasilisa, and, pushing open the front door, she stepped inside with the burning skull. To her great surprise, all three women were sitting in the dark. The magic the stepmother had used to kill the household's light had worked only too well. All the time Vasilisa had been away, no candle or torch could illuminate the house.

Eagerly the women rose to take the glowing skull. But now the skull came to life. With a will of its own, the head turned and focused its fiery eyes on the stepmother. Startled, she cried out and tried to flee. But the skull's gaze followed her, and again its blazing light fell upon her. In an instant she was engulfed in flames and quickly reduced to cinders. Then the eyes searched out each stepsister in turn, and they, too, were consumed by flames. In a great flash the light within the skull was extinguished. The room was thrown into darkness, with not a sound to be heard.

asilisa could not stay in the house another moment. She set out again, this time in the direction of the neighboring village.

At dawn, weary but resolute, she arrived. An elderly woman with no children of her own willingly took her in, and from that day forward Vasilisa's life changed for the good.

The years passed peacefully, and the old woman grew to look upon Vasilisa as her own dear daughter. Gone were the cruelties and the countless menial tasks of the past. In fact, the girl found she now had time to spare. Hating to be idle, she began spinning thread. The fabric she wove from it was like nothing ever seen before, it was so light and delicate. She folded it carefully and gave it all to the kindly old woman, insisting the gift was a token of her gratitude.

want you to take the fabric to the marketplace," Vasilisa told the old woman. "There I hope it will command a good price."

But the old woman could not bear to sell the fabric. No, she thought, it is far too rare and beautiful to sell. Indeed, it is fit only for the royal tzar himself. With that in mind she went to the tzar's palace and presented the exquisite cloth as a gift. The royal commissar accepted the cloth and sent it to the royal tailors to be cut and stitched into shirts for His Majesty.

"It's too fine," said the tailors when they saw it. "It would be impossible to cut such perfect fabric. His Majesty must send for the woman who made it. She, and no other, should cut the fabric."

So the old woman was summoned before the tzar and given the cloth to cut. But she refused, saying it was not her place to do it either, for she had not woven the fabric, that her adopted daughter must be asked, for she had spun the thread and woven it.

When Vasilisa came forward, the tzar fell in love at the sight of her. Forgotten was the cloth and the cutting and the stitching of the fabric. Vasilisa must be his wife, for he would have no other.

What happiness was theirs when Vasilisa consented. In a fortnight a magnificent wedding was celebrated with feasting and music and every kind of merriment.

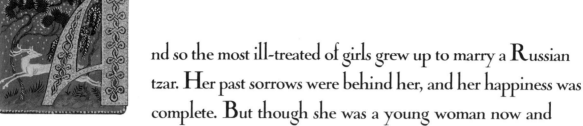

nd so the most ill-treated of girls grew up to marry a Russian tzar. Her past sorrows were behind her, and her happiness was complete. But though she was a young woman now and would live many a long year, Vasilisa never put aside her childhood friend, the little doll who had seen her through so much. Always she kept the little one close, and sometimes, on clear autumn nights when there was a certain crispness to the air, they were reminded of the ancient, the terrible Baba Yaga and would wonder what she was doing now.